Hank THE COWDOG®
AND MONKEY BUSINESS

John R. Erickson

Illustrations by Gerald L. Holmes

Maverick Books
Published by Gulf Publishing Company
Houston, Texas

This one is for Gary and Kim Rinker.

Maverick Books
Published by Gulf Publishing Company
P.O. Box 2608 Houston, Texas 77252-2608

10 9 8 7 6 5 4

Library of Congress Cataloging-in-Publication Data

Erickson, John R., 1943–
    Hank the Cowdog and monkey business/John R. Erickson;
illustrations by Gerald L. Holmes.
        p. cm.
    Summary: Hank the Cowdog, Head of Ranch Security,
matches wits with an escaped circus monkey.
    ISBN 0-87719-181-6.—ISBM 0-87719-180-8 (pbk.).—ISBN
0-87719-182-4 (cassette)
    1. Dogs—Fiction. [1. Dogs—Fiction. 2. Monkeys—Fiction.
3. Ranch life—Fiction. 4. Humorous stories.] I. Holmes, Gerald
L., ill. II. Title.
PS3555.R428H2796 1990
813'.54—dc20
[Fic]   90-13565
                                                              CIP
                                                              AC

Printed in the United States of America.

C O N T E N T S

Have you read all of Hank's adventures?
Available in paperback at $6.95:

All books are available on audio cassette too!
($15.95 for two cassettes)

Also available on cassettes:
Hank the Cowdog's Greatest Hits!

C H A P T E R

1

CHAPTER ONE ALWAYS PRECEDES CHAPTER TWO

It's me again, Hank the Cowdog. It was morning on the ranch, the beginning of another spring day. I had been up since before daylight, monitoring the forces of nature and guiding them through their morning routines.

While others sleep, the Head of Ranch Security is out there in the darkness, planning out the day. I had put in orders for the sun to come up in the east, and for a light dew to sprinkle the grass.

At 0700 hours, everything checked out. The sun and dew had followed my orders to perfection. At 0705 I issued a new set of orders, allowing the sun to rise in the sky, and the dew to begin sparkling on the grass.

1

At 0710, feeling pretty good about things, I made my way up to the machine shed. I had gotten another day off to a good start—or so it appeared. Little did I know that within a matter of hours, Drover and I would discover a Mysterious Red Box out in the pasture that would change the course of our lives.

Perhaps you don't believe in Mysterious Red Boxes. Well, that's too bad, because I found one on my ranch. Hang around and you'll see just how fast one of those things can turn a day around.

When I arrived at the machine shed, I found Drover sunning himself on the south side—sunning himself, gazing up at the clouds, and wasting time.

"Hi, Hank."

"Well, Drover, I see that you're sunning yourself, gazing up at the clouds, and wasting time."

He grinned. "Yeah, I get a kick out of that."

"You certainly do." I kicked him in the behind. "There's your kick. Now get up. We've got to make a Cattle Guard Patrol."

"But Hank . . ."

"Hush. And chase rabbits."

"Oh rats."

"Rabbits."

"Oh rabbits."

"What?"

"Nothing."

In security work we have certain jobs that we attend to every day, others that we take care of on a weekly basis. Cattle Guard Patrol falls into the latter category.

It's one of those jobs that has to be done every once in a while but not necessarily every day. It's important, but when we get involved with murder cases and reports of monsters on the ranch and other dangerous assignments, we tend to let the cattle guard work slide into the background.

We hadn't done a thorough Cattle Guard Patrol in several weeks and it was sure 'nuff time to do one. We went streaking past the chicken house, scattering chickens in all directions and barking, "Out of the way, you fools!"

I get a big kick out of scattering chickens, always have. It's a very satisfying part of my job. Give me two different routes to choose from, one clear and the other blocked by a bunch of chickens, and I'll take the chicken route every time.

There's something about the way they squawk and flap their wings that gives me a

G.L. Holmes

feeling of . . . something. Power. Total control. Superiority. It seems to tune up my savage instincts and get my blood to pumping.

Chickens were put on this earth to be scattered, and your better breeds of dogs rarely miss a chance to run through a crowd of them.

After plowing through the chickens and leaving them in squawking disarray, we continued on a northwesterly course out into the home pasture, and beyond to the country road. There we found the cattle guard, just where it had been the last time we'd patrolled it.

"All right, Drover, do you remember the procedure we follow on cattle guards?"

"Well, let's see. It's been a long time. Seems to me that we . . . bark?"

"That's correct up to a point, but also incorrect up to a point. Perhaps I should refresh your memory. Are you ready for me to outline our procedure for Cattle Guard Patrol?"

He yawned.

"What kind of answer is that?"

"It wasn't an answer. I just yawned."

"I know you yawned, you yo-yo, and you youldn't yoo yat."

"What?"

"I yaid, you yould yever yawn. . . ." Something had gone wrong with my talkatory mechanism. It had locked up on me.

Drover twisted his head and stared at me. "You sure are talking funny."

"Yes, and you yee what you've yone? You've yuined my yongue and made a yockery of my yecture! I yan't yalk or yive a yecture yith my yongue all yangled up yike yis, you yunce!"

"I don't know what you said, but I guess you're right."

5

I walked a short distance away and spit several times to get the knot out of my tongue. Sometimes, when you repeat certain sounds over and over, the muscle fibers in the tongualary region begin to cramp up, don't you see, causing the speaker to fixate on certain ridiculous sounds.

It's a humiliating affliction, and although we haven't found the exact cause, we know that it most often occurs when the victim is trying to communicate with morons. In the security business, we refer to it as *Tongue Runamuckus,* but there's no need for you to remember all the scientific terminography.

After a few moments, my tongue returned to its normal state and I marched back over to Drover.

"Point One: We know from our intelligence reports that a certain cottontail rabbit lives in the pipes of this cattle guard. Point Two: We also know that at this hour of the morning he leaves the pipes and ventures out into the pasture to feed on green grass. Point Three: It's our job to locate this rabbit while he's in a feeding mode. And, Point Four: Our mission is to cut off his attempts to scamper back into the safety of the pipes of the cattle guard. Is that clear?"

"Well . . . not really."

"Then never mind. We've got a job to do and you'll just have to play it by ear."

"What?"

"I said, you'll just have to play it by ear."

"What?"

"I said, you'll just have to . . . something must be wrong with your ear, Drover."

He pounded on the side of his head with a front paw. "Something's wrong with my ear."

"It's probably full of wax."

"No, I haven't seen any tacks."

I felt exhausted, dragged down into the dust by the forces of ignorance and anarchy. "Drover, look at me. Read my lips. Sometimes I think you're trying to make a mockery of my life."

"I must have some wax in this ear."

"And, Drover, sometimes I think I hate you."

"Hank, there's something I ought to tell you."

At last we were getting somewhere! The terrible truth had cut through the many layers of trash and had penetrated to the innermost garbage of his mind.

"Yes, Drover? Go ahead and make your confession. It'll hurt at first but in the long run, it'll hurt even worse. Just blurt it out in your own words."

"Hank, that little cottontail rabbit just crawled into the pipes of the cattle guard."

HUH?

My eyes darted from side to side, and slowly the pieces of the puzzle began falling into place. We had just been out-foxed by a rabbit, which was nothing to crow about.

CHAPTER
2

THE MYSTERIOUS RED BOX APPEARS

I turned my eyes back to Drover. "Well, are you happy now?"

"Oh, about the usual, I guess."

"You've ruined the exercise and made a shambles of our entire morning's work. The rabbit has entered the pipes of the cattle guard and now there's no chance that we'll get to chase him around."

"Well, I guess we can go back down to the gas tanks and catch up on our. . . ."

"Not so fast. Just because he gave us the slip doesn't mean we're going to quit and go home in disgrace. We'll just have to bark him out. Battle stations, Drover, and commence barking!"

We rushed to the north end of the cattle

guard. I began the procedure by peering into one of the pipes and sniffing it out.

"This is going to be easier than I thought. He's in this middle pipe. We've got him trapped, and now all we have to do is surround him."

"How do we do that?"

I removed my nose from the pipe and glared at him. "How do you think we do it, silly? A pipe has two openings, right? I have this opening covered and that leaves only one, right? Can you follow the logic to its conclusion or do I have to lead you to it?"

"Well, let's see. If you've got this end . . . maybe if I . . . I think I've got it. If I go down to the other end, we'll have him surrounded."

"Very good, Drover, only you forgot the most important part of the whole procedure: Drop your front end to the ground, elevate your little hiney, wag your tail and bark!"

"I don't have much of a tail to wag."

"That's correct. You may need to wag your hiney instead of your tail, since you have a stub tail."

"Yeah, that's what I meant."

"Exactly. Now let's go for it!"

Drover scampered across the road, dropped down into the correct barking stance, stuck his nose into the pipe, and began barking. 'did the same on my end and the exciteme'

Let me pause here to point out t into a cattle guard pipe isn't as might suppose. The problem is th mouth won't fit inside a four-in have to narrow our barking arc down to something in the range of two-and-a-half to three inches.

And still come out with a ferocious sound.

Pretty tough, huh? You bet it was, but we did it.

Five minutes into the procedure it occurred to me that something had gone wrong. Even though we had done some really spectacular barking, the rabbit was still inside the pipe.

I raised up and went through my check list and discovered . . . "Drover, you're barking in the wrong pipe! Move one pipe to the left."

"Oh, okay."

He did and we began the whole procedure over again from Step One. It took me another fifteen minutes to realize that we still had a flaw in the ointment.

"Drover, I said to move over one pipe to the *left*."

"I did."

"No, you moved over one pipe to the right. Right is wrong."

"I'll be derned. What's left in this old world if right is wrong?"

"Never mind the questions. Just move one ipe to the left and we'll get on with it."

shrugged and moved one pipe . . . .

"Drover, I told you to move to the *left*."

"I did."

"No, you moved to the right."

"No, I went left. See, here's my left paw."

He held it up. It appeared to be a left paw, all right, but how could that be? Something strange was going on here, and I went into deep concentration to find a solution.

"All right, Drover, I think I've found the missing piece of the puzzle. We're standing on opposite sides, you see. All we have to do is swap ends and your left will become right."

We swapped ends and both moved one pipe to the left and . . . hmmm, that was odd. This time we both ended up on the wrong. . . .

"Drover, I'm beginning to suspect that there's a mysterious magnetism in this cattle guard. It distorts the points of the compass and confuses our sense of direction."

"Yeah, but we don't have a compass."

"But if we had one, it would be distorted. The point is, with this heavy magnetic field at work, we'll have to change our tactics. This time, we'll put our noses into the *middle pipe*."

"Middle pipe. Okay, let's see here. The middle pipe would be the one in the middle?"

"That's correct. And once we direct both

13

our barkings into the same pipe, you see, the concentration of the sound will drive the rabbit out. Once he's outside, we'll catch him. Let's get after it!''

We put our noses into the pipe, the same pipe this time, and began the barking procedure all over again. I expected the rabbit to come out and surrender after a few minutes of this. But he didn't.

I withdrew my nose and sat down. "Drover, this isn't working."

"Yeah, I'm all discouraged now and ready to go back to bed."

"But the important thing is that we have him trapped. He'll have to come out of there sooner or later. He probably thinks that we'll give up and leave, but he doesn't realize with who or whom he's dealing. We'll just wait him out."

So we waited.

I hate to wait. It bores me to death. Your active minds find it hard to adjust to the slow rhythms of a nincompoop rabbit who has nothing better to do with his life than to sit inside a pipe and wiggle his nose.

The minutes crawled by. At last I could stand it no longer. I pushed myself up. "All right, we've completed Phase Two. Now we move into Phase Three. We'll change ends again and see if that helps."

We swapped ends, went through the barking procedure once again, and . . . at that point I began to face the possibility that we would have to rip into the steel pipe and destroy the entire cattle guard. I hated to take such drastic action but this rabbit was testing my patience.

So I took three steps backward and peered into the pipes one more time to confirm my visual. . . .

A truck was coming from the east. No, two trucks were coming from the east.

Three trucks.

Four.

Five.

A whole bunch of trucks. This was very strange. Seldom, if ever, had I seen so many trucks coming down our road at once. Someone on the creek must have been delivering a bunch of cattle that day, which meant that the approaching trucks were of the cattle truck variety.

"Drover, stand back and prepare to bark at these cattle trucks. As far as I know, they haven't been cleared to cross this ranch."

Each of us took a step or two backward,

crouched down, and prepared to give them the barking they so richly deserved. Here they came, a long line of trucks . . . that was odd. Painted red, white, blue, and yellow? With pictures of clowns and elephants and monkeys and people swinging on trapezes painted on the sides?

Hmmm.

"Drover, I'll want a complete description of every one of these trucks. I don't know what the neighbors are up to, but it's just possible that they've started raising elephants and clowns instead of cattle."

"I'll be derned."

The first truck was roaring down on us. "Ready for Heavy Duty Barking? Just a few more feet . . . okay, Drover, let 'em have it!"

When the front wheels of the first truck crossed the pipes of the cattle guard, we leaped out of the shadows, so to speak, and barked it from both sides. Pretty slick maneuver, caught 'em completely by surprise, and as you might expect, they didn't even dare to slow down.

The dust fogged around us but that didn't stop us from challenging the second truck, or the third. It was from the window of the third truck that the paper cup filled with ice came flying, hit me dead-center on the back, kind of shocked me there for a second.

I yelped but soon regained my composture, and by the time the back wheels of the truck crossed the cattle guard, I had jumped back into the struggle and torn most of the tread off the outside tire.

I mean, when they make me mad, they have to live with the consequences. I don't appreciate people throwing cups of ice at me when I'm on duty. They were just lucky I didn't get a good bite on that tire or I might have disabled the entire truck.

The dust boiled up, the trucks roared past and rumbled over our cattle guard, and we gave them a barking they would never forget. I had my doubts that they would ever risk coming down MY road again.

It's possible that the weight of the first five or six trucks mashed the cattle guard down, so that it was lower than the road. I say that because when the last truck came by, it bounced hard going over the cattle guard—so hard that a big red wooden box came loose from the top of the load and went flying off into the horse pasture.

I opened my mouth to alert Drover to this turn of events, but the swirling dust was so

thick that it filled my eyes and mouth with . . .
well, dust, of course. I coughed and spat and
waited for it to clear.

"All right, Drover, they're gone. Report in."

He sneezed. "It's dusty."

"That checks out. We had the same conditions over here."

"Yeah, 'cause it was the same bunch of
trucks."

"Exactly. Did we scare the liver out of those
guys or what ?"

"I didn't see any livers, but I think they
were scared."

"You bet they were scared! They'll think
twice before they come down our road again.
Oh, and did you notice that something fell off
that last truck?"

He moved out into the middle of the road,
sat down, and began scratching his ear. "Well,
I couldn't see because of the. . . ."

"A big red box fell off that last truck and
came to rest in our horse pasture. Stand by
with search parties! We're fixing to take possession of that box."

And with that, we leaped over the cattle
guard—well, most of it. I landed three pipes
short of the opposite side and lost a couple of

legs in the pipes, but that proved to be only a temporary setback.

Within seconds, we had located the Mysterious Red Box and had surrounded it.

CHAPTER

3

WE CAPTURE
THE BOX

Your ordinary dogs have no procedures or responses for Mysterious Red Box situations. I mean, to them a box is just a box, and they don't know what to do with it.

On this outfit, we have procedures and techniques and responses for just about any situation Life can throw at us, including but not limited to Mysterious Red Boxes that fall off of strangely painted cattle trucks.

Okay. It was lying in the grass, some fifty feet north of the road. I gave Drover orders to approach it from the south, while I circled around and came in from the north. You might be interested in hearing some of the more technical aspects of the capture, so I'll step it out for you.

Step One: Once in our positions, we went into the Stealthy Crouch Mode and began stalking towards the alleged box.

Step Two: Every third step we paused and barked a warning at the box. (A lot of dogs wouldn't take the time to do this, but it's very important. You never know what might be inside a box.)

Step Three: After each barst of burking, we crept forward again—burst of barking, I should say—with our auditory equipment poised to pick up any signals that might be transmitting from the box.

Step Four: At a distance of ten feet from the target, I gave the signal to Attack and Capture. We rushed forward from our respective positions, lifted our respective hind legs, and marked the box from our respective sides.

Step Five: Once marked, the box had become our possession, a trophy of war. But notice that we had done it all legal and proper, so there could be no argument about the change in ownership. We had by George marked it, and it was by George OURS.

I walked around and inspected Drover's side. "Nice work, son. That was a direct hit."

"Thanks, Hank. I think my aim's getting better. I used to miss every once in a while."

"Yes, and I remember a few occasions when you got so excited, you couldn't fire."

"Yeah, and I'd shoot myself in the leg about half the time."

"You've made real progress, but don't let it go to your head."

"Oh, my aim was never that bad."

"No, what I'm saying is, don't start thinking that you're a hot shot marksman and then get careless. Practice makes perfect."

"That's a good way to put it. 'Practice makes perfect.' Did you think that one up yourself?"

"Uh, yes, it's original, but you may quote me now and then if you wish. Just don't forget who said it first."

"Oh, I wouldn't do that." He sat down and grinned. "Well, we've got ourselves a nice big red box. What do you reckon we ought to do with it?"

I sat down and began admiring our new possession. "I can answer that question right quick. We'll roll it down to headquarters and set it up in our bedroom beneath the gas tanks. I've been thinking that we need something to liven up our bedroom."

"Yeah, me too. It's kind of drab."

"It's very drove, Drabber. The only question I have is, will a red box go with our color scheme?''

"You mean, with our gunny sacks and spills of diesel fuel?''

"Exactly, and with the silver tanks and the green pig weeds and the brown dirt?''

"Gee, I don't know about that.''

"Nor do I. We'll just try it and see. If we don't like it, we'll get rid of it and try something else.''

"Good idea. But it's a pretty big box. You think we can roll it all the way to the gas tanks?''

I gave him a sideward glance and smiled. "You saw what we did to those giant cattle trucks, didn't you? Do you suppose a box will cause us any trouble?''

"Well, I don't know. Are you sure those were cattle trucks?''

"Of course they were cattle trucks. What other kinds of trucks would pass down this road?''

"I don't know, Hank, but they were all painted up—kind of like circus trucks or something.''

"Don't be absurd. There are no circuses around here, hence, there can be no circus trucks. All that stuff painted on the sides was probably a clever disguise to keep us from barking at the trucks. But as you noticed, it didn't work."

"Sure didn't. I wasn't scared even a little bit."

"Just another cheap trick, Drover. Well, let's get this thing rolled down to. . . ."

That box was made out of three-quarter-inch plywood, and it was heavier than you might have thought.

"On second thought, Drover, I don't think we need a big red box in our bedroom."

"Yeah," he stopped pushing on the box and caught his breath, " 'cause we can't even budge it."

"That's correct, and budgets are crucial to ranch management. Let's leave her right where she lays."

"I'm for that. Hey, look. There's something written on the side of the box."

I moved around to the east side of the box and studied the large white letters. "Hmmm. You're right. Let's see if I can make it out."

WARNING! MONKEY!
DO NOT OPEN THIS BOX!

Drover was waiting for my translation. "What does it say, Hank? Can you read it?"

"Very interesting, Drover. In fact, VERY interesting. I've broken the code and translated the secret message."

"What does it say?"

"Give me a second to work it all out." I began pacing back and forth in front of the box, my mind moving outward into the realm of deepest concentration. "All right, I think I've got it. Drover, there's something inside this box that monkeys are not allowed to see."

"No foolin'?"

"That's correct. What tipped me off was the first line, which contains a warning to all monkeys. The only question remaining is, what could be hidden inside that monkeys are not allowed to have?"

"Well, let's see. Bananas?"

"Possibly so. Or peanuts? Or how about monkey wrenches? Yes, that's what it is. Drover, we have intercepted an illegal shipment of monkey wrenches!"

"You'd think they'd want monkeys to have monkey wrenches, wouldn't you?"

"Don't ever fall for the obvious, Drover. These people are clever beyond your wildest dreams. At this point we don't know why they want to keep the monkeys away from the monkey wrenches, but we have enough evidence to build a case. Now we must rush down to the house and sound the alarm."

"Or I guess we could open up the box and look inside. See, there's a wooden peg holding the hasp shut."

I turned to the runt and gave him a glare. "**Hasp?**"

"Yeah. The hasp is the thing that locks the door."

"Where did you learn that word?"

"Oh, I don't know, just picked it up somewhere."

"Well, I've never heard it before, and I don't appreciate you using big words around me."

"Oh, it's not so big, just a four-letter word."

"Exactly my point, and I've warned you about using four-letter words on the job. In security work, we have an image to protect, and nothing destroys an image faster than the casual, careless, indiscriminate use of four-letter words. Am I making myself clear?"

"Yeah."

"There's another four-letter word! Watch your step, Drover, before I have to take corrective measures."

"Okay."

"That's my last word on four-letter words."

"Good."

"Now, to the house. I think Sally May will want to know that we've discovered an illegal shipment of monkey wrenches in the horse pasture. Come on, let's fly!"

And with that, we made a dash back to headquarters to alert the house.

C H A P T E R

4

THE CAT BREAKS
DOWN UNDER
HEAVY INTERROGATION

We went roaring past the machine shed, past the chicken house, scattered chickens in all directions (I loved it!), past the water tank, and continued down the hill until we came to a stop in front of the yard gate.

There, we established a forward position and began barking. Boy, did we bark! I knew we'd get Sally May out of the house, and sure enough, before long the back door opened and she poked her head out.

"You dogs be quiet!"

HUH? Well, hey, there was a red box . . .

"Stop that barking right now!"

. . . out in the pasture, fell off a mysterious truck, an illegal shipment of . . .

29

"If you wake up the baby, I'll make you wish you hadn't!"

. . . but on the other hand, there was a time for serious barking and there was a time for serious non-barking, and it appeared that this might be a time to observe silence.

"Now, hush up!" The door slammed shut and Sally May went back into the house.

I turned to Drover and gave him a withering glare. "Why didn't you tell me the baby was asleep?"

"Well, I didn't know . . . I guess."

"Ignorance is no excuse. My mind is occupied with the larger matters of strategy and I expect you to keep up with the insignificant details."

"Well, if they're really insignificant, maybe. . . ."

"Don't argue with me. Just admit you were wrong and we'll go on from there."

"Oh, all right. I was wrong."

"There. Don't you feel better already?"

"Not really."

"I knew you would. Confession is good for all of us, Drover, but it's even better for you than for me. Try to remember that in the future."

"Okay. What are we going to do about the

box?"

Before I could answer, I noticed that a certain sniveling, sneaking, purring creature had joined us, and had begun rubbing up against Drover's leg. He tried to rub up against mine but I moved backwards and showed him some fangs.

I don't like cats, see, and I don't allow them to rub on my legs.

"Hi, Hankie. What you going to do about the box?"

"We're going to leave it just where it is, cat, and . . . wait a minute. How did you know about the box? That was Top Secret information."

Pete grinned and rubbed back and forth on Drover's leg. "Oh, I know just about everything, and I know you found a box."

"Oh yeah? We'll see about that. Was it a big red box made of three-quarter-inch plywood?"

"Um hmmm."

"Fell off a truck and landed out in the horse pasture?"

"Umm hmmm."

"Had white letters written on the side?"

"That's the one, Hankie."

I whirled around and faced Mister Spill-the-

Beans-and-Can't-Keep-a-Secret. "So! Now you're sharing secret inside information with the cat! What next, Drover? What new act of treachery can you find to top this one?"

"I didn't do it, Hank, honest I didn't. I've been with you the whole time."

"Hmm, that's true." I whirled back around and turned my cold, steely eyes on the spy. "You're lying, cat. Drover couldn't have possibly leaked that information to you, because he's been with me the entire morning. I've trapped you in a lie, and now I want the whole story. How did you know about the Mysterious Red Box?"

He took his sweet time in answering. He arched his back, yawned, stretched, and dug his claws into the ground. "We cats are very clever, Hankie. We know just about everything. Would you like for me to tell you what was written on the side of the box in white letters?"

"Huh? Wait a minute! How did you know about the white letters?"

"How I know doesn't matter, Hankie. Would you like for me to tell you what the letters said?"

I took a step forward, growled, and gave him a shove. "No, I wouldn't. I saw it first, and if somebody's going to talk about it, I'll be that somebody. It's MY box."

"You shouldn't be so selfish, Hankie. Someone who didn't know you might think you were rude, crude, uncouth, and socially unacceptable."

"Oh yeah? Let's put it this way, cat. I'm crude and proud of it. And while we're at it, let's put it another way. It's my box and I'll do the talking about what was written on the side. You got that?"

He grinned and purred and flicked the end of his tail. "Whatever you think, Hankie."

"It said, 'Warning! Monkey! Do Not Open This Box.' So there you are, cat. Once again, I've beat you to the punch and exposed you as the fraud that you are. How does it feel to be on Life's Second String?"

"Sometimes it's hard to bear, but we do the best we can."

I snorted at that. "Your so-called **best** would get you thrown off my security force in record time, kitty. You wouldn't last five minutes in my outfit.

"Yeah," said Drover, "and we don't let cats in our outfit anyway, so there."

"Well said, Drover." I patted the little mutt on the back. He doesn't often come up with a stinging retort that really stings, but I thought that one was pretty good.

We stood together, Drover and I, two proud members of an elite outfit. We held our heads high and smirked down at the cat.

He licked his paw and looked up at us with big lazy eyes. "Well, Hankie, are you going to let the monkey out of the box?"

Drover and I exchanged glances and started laughing. "Hey, Drover, did you hear that?"

"Yeah, I heard it but I don't believe it."

"Where has this cat been all his life?"

"I don't know, but he didn't go to the same school we went to, did he?"

"No, he didn't, Drover, and I have my doubts that he could have even gotten in the front door."

"Yeah, or the back door either."

"Exactly. As a matter of fact. . . ." I stopped laughing. I cut my eyes from side to side. I looked down at the cat. He was still licking his paw. "What makes you think there's a monkey in that box?"

"Because, Hankie, that's what the sign said: 'Warning! Monkey! Do Not Open This Box.' "

Drover was still giggling. "Oh, that's a good one! A monkey in the box! Pete doesn't know about the monkey wrenches, does he?"

34

"Quiet, Drover, I'm thinking." I pushed myself up and began pacing in front of the cat— also watching him out of the corner of my eye. "I'll need to ask you a few questions, cat, and I expect brief, factual answers, not your usual trash."

"Oh good! I just love questions."

"Number One: Do you know now, or have you ever known, the meaning of the word 'hasp?' "

"Oh, but of course, Hankie. Anyone knows that a hasp is used to secure the lid on a box. And I'll bet there's even one on the monkey box."

"Just answer my questions, cat. You can show off on your own time. Number Two: If you were shipping wrenches across country, would you pack them in a big red wooden box with a hasp on the lid?"

"Oh, that's a tough one." He flexed his claws and studied them for a moment. "No, I wouldn't, Hankie. But if I were shipping a monkey across country," he grinned, "I would."

"Just as I suspected!" I stopped pacing and glared back at Drover. "You idiot, that box doesn't have wrenches in it. There's a monkey in there—a real live monkey!"

"Well, I . . . but you said. . . ."

"Never mind the excuses, Drover. We deal in facts, not excuses, and the fact is that you came very close to bungling another investigation." I paced back to the cat. "One last question and then you're excused." I glanced over both shoulders and lowered my voice to a whisper. "How much do you know about monkeys?"

"Well, a little bit, Hankie, but nothing you'd be interested in hearing."

"Out with it, before I lose my patience."

He spent a moment admiring his claws. "They're cute. They're smart. They can do things with their little hands. They can be trained to perform tricks if . . ."

"Yes? Go on."

". . . if the master is smarter than the monkey." He fluttered his eyes and began rubbing up against my leg. "Would you like some good advice, Hankie?"

"No. I don't take advice from cats. You're excused."

"If I were you. . . ."

"But you're not me. Too bad for you and good-bye. Scram. Get lost. Go chase your tail."

And with that, Pete the Barncat left the interrogation room in complete disgrace. With just a few savage thrusts, I had broken him down, wrung the truth out of him, and exposed him as a sneak, a liar, and a pompous fraud.

"Well, Drover, that just about wraps up the Case of the Mysterious Red Box. As you might have guessed by now, we have come into possession of a circus monkey."

"A circus monkey!" Drover shook his head and walked around in a small circle. "I'm all confused. Why would a circus monkey be riding on a cattle truck?"

I glared at the runt. "Drover, who's running this outfit?"

"Well, let's see. You?"

"That's correct. And who asks all the questions around here?"

"Uh . . . you?"

"Correct again. Did I ask anything about cattle trucks?"

"I don't think so."

"Therefore, there is no question about cattle trucks. The only question before us at the moment is, what will we do with the monkey?"

"Oh, that's easy. We'll leave him in the box. I don't want a monkey running around here . . . do you?"

I gave him a veiled smile. "Of course not, Drover. Of course not."

C H A P T E R

5

A STRANGER EMERGES FROM THE BOX

As soon as possible, I sent Drover on a mission to patrol the eastern quadrant of ranch headquarters. He didn't want to go and came up with the usual excuses: His leg hurt, his sinuses were bothering him, and there was no particular reason for going on patrol in the light of day.

On the last score, he happened to be right. What he didn't know was that I wanted to get rid of him for a while because, shall we say, I had some other business to attend to.

When he was out of sight, I turned to the west and went streaking away from headquarters and out into the horse pasture. By that time I had begun conducting a serious debate within the inner sanctum of my mind: Did I want to release the monkey or did I not?

Or to phrase it another way: Was there actually a monkey in the box or was there not? For you see, if there was no monkey in the box, the question of whether or not to release him became mute. Mutt. Mood. Moot, I suppose it is.

The question became mute. Therefore, the logical sequence of events would be for me to determine . . . I think you get the drift.

I reached Point X very shortly after leaving hindquarters . . . headquarters, that is . . . and found the box exactly where we had left it. In other words, it hadn't moved. I approached it with caution, sniffed it out, barked at it, and circled it three times, with each circle bringing me closer to it.

At last, satisfied that it wasn't going to move or spring at me or do anything of a suspicious nature, I spoke to it:

"The voice you're hearing belongs to Hank the Cowdog, Head of Ranch Security. You are trespassing on my ranch, which means that you have gotten yourself into serious trouble.

"If you are in there and can hear my voice, I demand that you come out immediately and identify yourself. If you're not in there, you may disregard this message."

I lifted my ears to the Full Alert position and waited. At first I heard nothing. Then . . . a scratching sound? Yes! A certain scratching sound, as though someone or something were scratching on the inside of the alleged box.

Did it scare me? Well . . . a little bit, might as well admit it, okay, yes, maybe it scared me a little bit, but after running backwards for twenty or thirty yards, I regained my poise and approached it again.

"I'll repeat the message one more time," I said in my firmest voice. "We have your box surrounded. There's no chance of escape or any other kinds of mischief. You will come out of the box and identify yourself at once."

More scratching from inside the box, and oh yes, the hasp.

Let me pause here to point out that your heavy boxes, such as the type used to transport circus animals, often have a device on the lid called a **hasp.** Hasp is a technical term, you've probably not run into it before, but we use it all the time in the security business.

A hasp secures the lid to the box, see, and until I removed the wooden peg from the eye of the hasp, the lid would not open.

Okay. We had gotten down to the meat of the heart . . . the core of the meat . . . the heart of the core . . . the central issue in the whole deal. DID I WANT TO OPEN THE DOOR AND RELEASE THE MONKEY, OR WHATEVER IT WAS, ONTO MY RANCH?

If you've fooled around with geometry, you know that there are three sides on a pyramid, three legs on a triangle, four legs on a donkey, and two sides to every question. Before moving any closer to the box, I pondered both sides of this particular question.

On one side, we had yes. Immediately across from it, on the other side, we had no. Yes and no are not only spelled differently, but they don't mean the same thing. In fact, they are diabolically opposed. Thrown together in a small space, they will fight until only one emerges the winner. Hence, by simple logic, it followed that I could not possibly decide both yes and no on the same question. It had to be one or the other.

For several minutes the argument raged back and forth in my mind. "Yes. No. Yes! No! Yes yes! No no!" As you can see, the argument began to tilt in favor of yes. 'Yes,' being a three-letter word, carried exactly one-third more weight than 'no,' which was a two-letter word.

The longer the argument raged, the more

42

weight accumulated on the yes-side, until at last the scales of justice could no longer resist the weight of reason, and the balance tipped in favor of yes.

Oh, and there was one other small factor: The lettering on the side. It said, "Do Not Open This Box!" I have never taken orders from a box, and I never will. No box tells Hank the Cowdog what he can do on his own ranch.

I marched forward, hopped my front legs up on the top of the device, and proceeded to remove the wooden peg from the hasp.

At that moment, I was greeted, if that's the proper word, by the thunder of hooves. It caught me completely by surprise, I mean, it

WARNING
MONKEY
DO NOT OPEN
THIS BOX

sounded like a whole herd of horses was coming out of that box.

Oh. I was in the horse pasture, so to speak, and so it was natural that . . . what I'm driving at here is that the horses had seen me out there in their pasture and had come thundering over to check things out.

They are curious brutes, you see, and very snotty and possessive about their pasture. They have never recognized my jurisdiction in their territory, and they seldom pass up a chance to torment me when I enter it.

I may have mentioned this before, but I don't like horses at all, and I have every reason to suppose that they don't like dogs either.

Well, here they came—snorting, bucking, laughing, and grinning with those big ugly awkward green-stained teeth of theirs. I'd drawn the whole crowd: Popeye, Casey, Chief, Cookie, Happy, Deuce, Frisco, Calypso, Bonny Bonita, Lightning, every stinking horse on the ranch.

And before I could run, they had me surrounded. The first to speak was Casey, the smartest aleck of all the smart alecks.

"Say, puppy dog, you in the wrong place, and you fixin' to wish you was in the right place." They all got a big laugh out of that.

"We got a law against dogs in the horse pasture, and son, you have broke the law!"

To which I made a brilliant and stinging reply: "Oh yeah?"

"You know what we do when we catch puppy dogs on our side of the fence? We tough, son. We tear up a dog like a Dixie cup."

I tried a different approach. "Oh yeah?"

"Oh yeah. And we love it too. And now . . ."

At that very precise moment, the lid on the box flew open and a hairy little man in a red fez and a red jacket popped out, screamed and waved his arms at the horses, and **jumped on my back.**

Two things happened real quick. First, fourteen head of saddle horses dropped their heads, lifted their ears, widened their eyes, snorted, and headed for the south end of the pasture in a dead run.

Second, I did exactly the same thing, heading in the opposite direction. I figgered that anybody who was dangerous enough to scare fourteen head of horses didn't belong on my back, or anywhere close.

I ran, I bucked, I twisted, I barked, I did everything I could think of to get him off me, but he must have been a professional bronc

G.L. Holmes

rider because I couldn't shake him loose. Not
only did he have a good grip with his legs, but
he was also using my ears for bridle reins.

I bucked until I couldn't buck any more, ran
until I couldn't run another step, barked until
I was completely out of breath. And at that
point, fellers, I knew I'd been beat and that I
belonged to that bronc-riding son of a gun in
the red hat.

I stopped to catch my breath. "Okay, you win. I surrender. I don't know who you are, pal, but you've sure taken the fire out of this old dog."

He climbed off my back and said something in a strange, squeaky voice: "Eee eee." I noticed that he had a tail, a wide mouth, kind of a monkey-looking face, fingers and thumbs on his feet and. . . .

Come to think of it, if you'd taken away his coat and hat, he would have looked a lot like a . . . hmmmmm.

You probably thought he was a hairy little man in a red jacket and fez, who bore a passing resemblance to a monkey. I might have made that mistake too, had I not been armed with the stern discipline of a trained observer.

He was a monkey, see, not a man at all. I had suspected . . . there for a second he did look a little bit. . . .

At last I had cleared up the mystery. As I had surmised, the box had contained a circky monkus. A circus monkey, that is. And the next step was to open lines of communication with the little brute and to establish whether I was working for him or if he was working for me.

That was kind of an important question, see.

47

6

I TAKE CHARGE OF THE MONKEY

I caught my breath and then addressed him. "You are a monkey, is that correct?"

"Eee eeee."

"I don't know much about monkeys, so we'll need to establish some lines of authority here. I notice that you have sharp teeth, as well as a pair of hands that can wield a club or a rock. So I guess our basic question here is, are you taking over my ranch?"

He just stared at me and grinned. He didn't appear as ferocious now as he had when he'd come out of the box and scared the horses. I decided to test him. I stood up and began walking around.

"Of course, another way of looking at the deal—I'm not saying this is the way it has to be, understand, just throwing out ideas—is that you're on my ranch. One possible interpretation is that you've come under the authority of the Security Division. How does that grab you?"

He grinned and clapped his hands.

When I spoke again, I could hear boldness creeping back into my voice. "As a matter of fact, that's exactly what has happened. You're on my ranch and I happen to be in charge here —unless, of course, you have serious objections to that."

He stuck one of his little humanoid fingers into his left ear and drilled out some wax. My impression was that he was buying my program.

I began swaggering back and forth in front of him. "Okay, let my lay out some basic rules of behavior. We'll try to get you back to the circus as soon as possible, but in the meantime, you are on MY ranch, do you understand that?"

"Eee eee."

"While you're on my ranch, you will follow my orders and do as I say. Is that clear?"

He jumped up and down and clapped his hands. This was going better than I had expected.

"I get the feeling that you kind of like the idea of taking orders from me, is that correct?" Again, he clapped his hands. "Well, let's talk about that. I have no use for monkeys or anyone else who can't take orders, who grumbles when asked to do certain jobs, or who questions my authority."

This time, the little rascal did a back flip. I mean, he was just by George beside himself about meeting the H.D.I.C. (Head Dog In Charge). I continued pacing.

"On other outfits, the same job as mine would carry the title of King, Emperor, Caesar, or Grand Potentate. We use the more modest Head of Ranch Security, but don't let that fool you. I carry a lot of weight around here."

The monkey clapped and grinned and hopped up and down.

"While you're here on the ranch, you should feel free to think of me as the Grand Potentate." He liked that! "Or, the Great Grand Potentate, if you prefer." He liked that even better!

"Speaking of which, I just happen to have a position open on my staff. I'm looking for a guy with absolute loyalty and unquestioned obedience. I've never hired a monkey before, but. . . ." I stopped pacing, turned suddenly, looked him square in the eyes, and said, "How would you like to go to work for me, son?"

I had never seen a happier monkey. He ran around in a circle, did handsprings and cartwheels, and ended the whole thing by bowing before me and saying, "Eee eee! Eee eee!"

Fellers, that was good enough for me. I hired him on the spot.

I looked down at the little guy and couldn't help smiling. I mean, I had made him SO HAPPY!

Here was a poor little monkey who was lost and alone, who'd been torn from his home and cast out into the cold, cruel world, who had no chance to advance or improve himself or use his talents, who'd been locked in a dark prison until I came along and flang open the doors of freedom.

Hey, if you can't make somebody happy in this old world, you might as well be somewhere else . . . although I don't know where else you'd go, come to think of it.

But the point is, I had brought absolute happiness to this monkey while at the same time solving a small problem of my own—namely, replacing a certain grumbling, begrudging, half-stepping, gold-bricking, hypocardiac little mutt as my First Assistant.

It was shaping up to be a heck of a deal.

"All right, Monkey, now let's get down to the conditions of your employment. Sit." He sat, instantly, and I mean, I had his full attention. I liked that. "Here is a brief job description. You will attend to every tiny whim and desire of your master. Is that clear?"

He rippled his lips and clapped.

"Every morning, you will bring a bowl of dog food to my bed. Then, while I'm eating, you will pick the grass stems, weed seeds, and stickers out of my coat. When I rise from my bed, you will snap to attention, do a backward flip, lift your hat three times, and then slap yourself hard on both cheeks. Try it once. Let's see if you can do it."

Hey, this was a good monkey! He remembered the whole routine and followed it to the letter.

"Very good, Monkey, although in actual practice, I'll want you to slap yourself a little harder than that. It's to remind you that, in the grand scale of things, you're really not much."

You know what that monkey did then? He SLUGGED himself with each fist, and I mean, slugged himself so hard that it knocked him down!

"That's more like it! You bet, that's okay,

just right. I like the way you do things, Monkey. Now, one last thing. When I tell you, 'The Great Grand Potentate will now sit,' I'll expect you to have the ground swept clean before my hams touch down.''

His face brightened. He nodded his head and went through the sweeping procedure. I walked over and examined the ground.

"Could be cleaner, but not bad for the first time out. I think we're ready to make our first appearance down at headquarters. You will go in front and clear my path of chickens, cats, and other obnoxious creatures. I will come along behind. Do you understand Us?''

He clapped his hands and nodded his head.

"Very good. Oh, before we set out, why don't you slap yourself around a few more times, just to be sure you've got it."

Say, that monkey got after the program, slugged himself so hard on the chin that it knocked him out! I had to shake him a few times to bring him around.

"That was just right. I think you've got the idea. We will now proceed to ranch headquarters. Oh, one last thing, Monkey." I placed a paw on his shoulder and spoke to him in a voice that was heavy with sincerity. "I'd rather the people at the house didn't see you. They might try to send you back to your cruel master in the circus. Now that we've won your freedom, we don't want to take any chances of losing it. It's, uh, for your own good, do you understand?"

He nodded and said, "Eee eee."

We set out for headquarters. Monkey went in front, walking on all-fours part of the time and on his hind legs part of the time. It was clever, the way he could do that. When he wasn't looking, I tried it myself and it didn't work.

As we rounded the west side of the machine shed, Monkey, as I called him, made his first contact with the chicken-rabble. I watched him carefully to see how he handled them.

The first chicken he came to was pecking gravel and paying no attention to world events. My monkey fixed her by pulling five large feathers from her tail and then booting her out of the way. Her squawking was music to my ears.

The other chickens scattered, leaving Us a clear path to the front of the machine shed. There, We halted the procession. "We will pause here, Monkey, so that We might address the rabble. The Great Grand Potentate will sit."

Sure enough, before Our royal bohunkus touched the ground, Monkey had it swept clean. The ground, not the bohunkus.

We cleared Our throat and looked around at the circle of chickens, who were watching Us rather carefully now.

"We have a message to deliver: You are all lowly scum and you will not clutter Our path. Those chickens who disregard Our commandment will be dealt with by Our captain of the guards. We will now proceed forward, Monkey."

We rose from Our sitting position, and Captain Monkey swept the particles of dirt and so forth from Our backside.

The procession resumed, winding its way down towards the gas tanks, but as We passed in front of the machine shed, Our glance happened to fall upon a certain smirking, insolent face in the crowd.

"Halt! Monkey, come here!" He came back to Us in a run. We liked the way he hustled when We called his name. "Monkey, you see that cat basking in the sun over there? He isn't showing Us the proper respect. Can you think of some way of calling this to his attention?"

Monkey grinned and a wicked little twinkle came into his eyes, something I hadn't noticed before. I had a feeling that with the proper training and direction, this monkey could turn out to be a dangerous weapon.

"Get the cat and bring him to Us!"

Monkey bounded over to the machine shed doors. When Pete saw him coming, he rose to his feet, pinned back his ears, threw a hump into his back, and began to hiss and yowl. Monkey's answer to that was very simple: He snatched Pete up by the tail and brought him to me—Us, I should say.

"Eee eee!"

"Well done, Monkey." We smirked and looked into Pete's dark eyes. "In the future, cat, when Our procession files past, you will

G.L. Holmes

stand at attention and show Us the proper respect. Failure to do so will result in your being seized by the Captain of the Guard."

Pete hissed and yowled and clawed the air.

"Monkey," We said, "spank him!"

With what you might describe as devilish glee, the monkey proceeded to deliver three swats to Kitty-Kitty's backside, while We watched and gloated and chuckled. It was one of Our better moments on the ranch.

"Release the swine," We ordered, "and proceed forward! To the gas tanks, Monkey."

Once again, the procession began to move through the central plaza of ranch headquarters. Pete the Barncat observed the rest of the parade from one of the lower branches of the nearest elm tree, into which he had climbed upon being released by the Captain of the Guard.

If looks could have killed, We would have suffered mortal wounds from the cat. Oh, Kitty-Kitty was stirred up!

The procession wound through the Central Plaza and made its way down the hill to the gas tanks. Our feathered subjects, the chickens, lined the streets. As We passed, they bowed and whispered, "'Tis HE, the Great Grand Potentate!"

We had planned to take a short nap upon reaching the Royal Gas Tank Throne Room, but Our nap was delayed because of trouble from an unexpected source: Drover.

CHAPTER

7

MONKEY SEE, MONKEY DO

If you recall, We had assigned Drover a routine patrol job in the eastern quadrant of ranch headquarters. We found him asleep on his gunny sack—in Our Gas Tank Throne Room.

We extended Our paw toward the offender. "Monkey, seize him!"

Monkey chattered with sheer delight, jumped into the middle of the sleeping goldbricker, and pinned him to his bed. Drover received a rude awakening, and when he saw what was sitting astraddle of him, his eyes became large white plates with little black dots in their centers.

"Hank, oh my gosh, mayday, mayday, help, murder!" We floated into the Throne Room

61

and seated Ourself upon the Royal Gunny Sack Throne. "Hank, who is this guy? Get him off me!"

"Silence! You disturb Our tranquility."

"What's going on? Who . . . oh my gosh, Hank, I've got a monkey on me!"

We smiled and fingered the large emerald ring upon Our paw. "Drover, you have disobeyed Us, and as a result you have been seized by Our Captain of the Guard."

"Who? Hank, where'd you get . . . oh. I bet you opened the box, didn't you, and there was a monkey inside. Oh good! There for a minute, I thought I was having a bad dream. Can you get him off of me?"

"We could, Drover, but We won't."

"We? Who's we?"

"We. We, the Great Grand Potentate of the Ranch."

Drover gave me a silly grin. "What are you talking about? You must be . . . I hope you're . . . I think I missed something."

"Yes, indeed. While you slept, Drover, many things happened. We have been crowned Great Grand Potentate of the Ranch, and Our monkey has been named Captain of the Guard and second in command."

"Second in . . . what about me?"

"You are now third in command. Or last in command, as it were."

"You mean. . . ."

"Exactly. In the future, you will take orders from Captain Monkey. You will also accept his punishment for sleeping on the job."

"But Hank, this leg of mine. . . ."

"Monkey, pull his whiskers and tweak his nose!"

"Eee eee!" Monkey did as he was told. I could see that he enjoyed his work.

"Oh, ouch, quit that, Hank, get him off of me! He's pulling my whiskers."

"Exactly. And now you will thank him for improving you."

"Thank him for . . . Hank, are you feeling all right? He just pulled my whiskers and. . . ."

We leaped up from Our throne. "**You will thank Captain Monkey for improving you, or We will order him to improve you some more!**"

"Well, you'd better do that, 'cause I'm not going to thank any monkey for pulling my whiskers."

Our lip curled and we glared down at the little mutt. "Insolent wretch. Very well. As you have spoken it, so shall it be." We floated over to Captain Monkey and whispered something in his ear.

What I whispered in his ear was Top Secret Procedure for subduing and gaining control of a dog, any dog, regardless of how big or mean or stubborn he might be. I had never revealed this secret to anyone, not even to Drover, and for very good reason. Such a secret, once revealed, can become a double-edged blade in the razor of Life. Not only can it shave closer and faster, but it can. . . .

Let's back up and start over. Such a secret, once revealed, can be used by small minds against the revealer, if the revealer happens to be a dog, don't you see. I wouldn't have taught the trick to just anyone, but by this time I had established that the monkey was my loyal and obedient subject. Also not shrewd enough to use it against me.

Do I dare reveal the secret here? No, better not risk it. Or, I'll tell you what, we'll make a deal. I'll reveal the secret if you'll raise your right hand and swear never to tell anyone else or use it against a dog.

Okay. Raise your right hand and repeat after me: "I, your name, do solemnly swear never to repeat this Top Secret Procedure to anyone or to use it against an innocent dog."

Now we're set. Are you ready to hear the

secret? Here it is. **If you want to shut down and humble a dog, grab his tongue and hold on. As long as you have that tongue, he can't talk back, bite, bark, or do ANYTHING.**

There it is, the secret I whispered in my monkey's ear. Don't forget that you've sworn an oath never to repeat it.

Now, back to the story. When We had revealed this Utmost Dark Secret to the monkey, he grinned from ear to ear, and once again We saw that wicked gleam shining in his eyes.

We returned to Our throne and seated Ourselves. "Now, Drover, you will thank Captain Monkey for aiding you in your quest for self-improvement."

"Well, I really don't think I want to lum wum wug lum wum."

We smiled. "Drover, We're afraid We missed the last part of your statement. Could you say it again, a little louder this time?"

"Lum wum wug lum wum lum lum."

"Mercy! It seems Captain Monkey has seized you by the tongue and rendered you helpless. Could this be a message of sorts, hmmm?"

"Lum wum wug."

"So it seems. When your little rebellion has passed and you're ready to follow orders, give

Us a sign and We will issue the command for Captain Monkey to release your tongue."

Several minutes passed, while Drover lummed and wummed and mummed in protest, but his protests didn't do a lick of good, so to speak, because my monkey kept a good grip on his tongue. At last, Drover crossed his eyes, which I figgered was the sign that he was ready to give up.

"Monkey, release the scoundrel's tongue." That was odd. The monkey shook his head and scowled, almost as though he didn't understand the order—or didn't want to understand the order.

We pushed Ourself up from the Royal Gunny Sack Throne and marched over to him. "Your master has spoken: Release the tongue, chop-chop, boola-boola, right now!"

This time he did as he was told, but with a certain air of resentment that I didn't . . . I salted this clue away for future reference. Unless I was badly mistaken, my loyal monkey showed signs of having thoughts of his own.

There are several things you look for in a good monkey, and thoughts of his own ain't one of them.

We would deal with the monkey later, but at the moment Our most pressing problem was curbing Drover's little outburst of rebellion.

"Are you ready now to repent, O Lowly One?"

"I guess, but I didn't like. . . ."

"What you like or dislike is of no concern to Us. Thank Captain Monkey."

Drover scowled and pressed his lips together in a pout. "Thank you, Captain Monkey, for your help in making me a better dog."

"Excellent! Let him up, Monkey. We have guided him through the dark night of rebellion and around the sharp rocks of . . . I said, LET HIM UP, MONKEY."

That same grudging look. I didn't like it. Obviously, I needed to do some more work on this monkey, and I made a mental note to attend to it first thing after my nap.

Drover scrambled to his feet and began backing away from Us. "I said it, Hank, but I don't like it, and I don't like your monkey either, and I'm sorry you let him out of the box and I think you're going to be sorry too."

Captain Monkey snarled and made a move towards Little Mister Talk-Back-When-He-Ought-To-Keep-His-Trap-Shut. We had to step between them to keep Captain Monkey from teaching him another painful lesson.

"You may leave, Drover. Go contemplate

your naughty behavior. Next time, We won't let you off so easy. Off with you! Be gone!"

"All right, I'll go, but I still don't like that monkey."

I made a move towards him and he made a lightning dash for the machine shed. I yawned, feeling tired all at once from the strains of governing my unruly kingdom, and returned to my. . . .

The monkey was sitting on my throne. And grinning.

"Get off my throne, you flea-bitten circus clown, and don't go near it again! For that, We command you to slap yourself three times and stand in the corner until We have taken our royal nap."

That was more like it. He slapped himself three times on the face and placed his nose in the corner of the northeast angle-iron leg of the gas tanks.

We fluffed up Our gunny sack, walked around it in a tight circle, and flopped down. Oh, wonderful gunny sack! Oh, delicious sleep!

I stretched out, wiggled around until I found a comfortable spot and had all four paws sticking up in the air, closed my eyes, and began drifting off. . . .

Ah, sweet Beulah, of the flaxen hair and soft brown eyes! Collie girl of my dreams, love of my life, giver of all good things, source of inspiration and happiness!

I glimpsed her in the distance, in the fog, in the foggy distance. I could see the longing in her eyes. I called her name and she called mine. We ran towards each other, our hearts aflame, but the fog rolled between us.

"Beulah!"

"Hank!"

"Oh, Beulah!"

"Oh, Hank!"

"Oh, Beulah, oh!"

"Oh, Hank, oh!"

And just then, I heard music. A song, in fact. It went like this.

I Can See You Now

I can see you now, just the way you
    were when daylight found you.
I can see you now, with the morning's
    golden glory all around you.
I can see the wind's soft fingers running
    through your hair,
The amber light reflected in your eyes.

I can see the fields of flowers like a
  rainbow
Splashed across the earth and stretching
  to the skies.

I can see you now, just the way you
  were when evening found you.
I can see you now, with the purple
  shadows falling all around you.
I can see the wind's cool fingers running
  through your hair,
And evening stars reflected in your eyes.
I can see bright colors fading all around
  you,
As night's blue velvet veil is drawn
  across the skies.

I can see you now, just the way you
  were when darkness found you.
I can see you now, but the memory
  starts to fade as night surrounds you.
I can hear you calling to me in the
  darkness,
I hear the words but don't know what
  they mean.
I can see stars in your eyes like burning
  embers,

But just before the dawn, I wake and it's
a dream.
I see you now.
I see you now.
I see you now.

CHAPTER

8

THE PASHA
OF SHIZZAM

It was, to say the least, a bittersweet dream, which sort of describes the way things have gone with Beulah from the very beginning. If that bird dog would just go away . . . oh well. I don't want to get started on Plato.

Except to say that any dog who chases birds can't be very smart, and any woman who chases bird dogs, when she could have a brave, magnificent Great Grand Potentate cowdog for the same price, is walking the fine line between poor taste and terrible judgment.

But I don't want to get started on that. There's no rational explanation for it, that's what torques me about the whole thing. I mean, is there anything dumber or less significant than pointing birds? Who cares about birds? If you're going to point something, point something that matters. That's what I always say.

But never mind. I can't be bothered . . . what is it about that stupid, spotted, stick-tailed bird dog that holds her interest day after day, week after week, and month after month? It's outrageous.

But the important point to remember in all this is that **I really don't care.** There are other women in the world, hundreds of them, thousands of them, and if she wants to go chasing after a stupid . . . phooey!

Nevertheless, it was a wonderful dream, in a painful sort of way, and I wouldn't have minded running it over and over through the entire afternoon and into the evening hours. But that wasn't to be. Drover, the little dunce, began pulling my ears.

When I felt the first tug at my left ear, I growled, pretty muchly on instinct, and told him, "Drover, you're dlvkskdi bchslek vksl."

"That wasn't me, Hank. You'd better wake up and see. . . ."

"And you'd better zvlsckelf b'aldke mfkd ake zzzzzz."

"Hank, get up. Somebody's here."

"Of course somebody'zzzzzz snort wheeze

74

here, otherwise we wouldn't be talking to each other."

"No, I mean somebody else."

"Tell 'em I'm busy. Tell 'em I died three weeks ago. Tell 'em. . . ." He pulled my ear again. "Tell 'em that if you pull my ear again, you nincompoop, I'm going to build a mud-hole in the middle of your face!"

He pulled it again. That did it. My eyelids sprang open, and once my eyeballs quit rolling around and locked in on the target, I saw . . .

HUH?

. . . this face, see: Two big eyes, short nose, a broad grinning mouth, jug ears, red jacket, and a red fez on top of its head. Drover didn't wear a red fez. Or have jug ears. Or a short nose.

"Drover, I don't want to alarm you, but something has happened to your face. All at once it has begun to resemble a. . . ."

"A monkey, Hank?"

"Exactly. All these years you've acted like a monkey, and now the chickens have come home . . . Drover, is there something we need to discuss?"

"Yeah. I think your monkey's got some business on his mind."

"Which could be called monkey business, is

that what you're saying?''

"Yeah. He's sitting on your chest. I told him to get off but he only made teeth at me and stuck out his tongue.''

"I see. Yes, it's all coming clear now. I gave him strict orders to stand with his nose in the corner. He has disobeyed, and now we have the Case of the Disobedient Monkey.''

"I guess so. What are you going to do?''

"Very simple, Drover. Obviously the little whelp has forgotten his place in the overall scheme of things and must be taught a lesson. I'll simply order him to get off my chest.''

"That sounds like a good idea—if he'll do it.''

"He'll do it. I'll speak to him in his own dialect. Watch this and study your lessons.'' I beamed a steely gaze into the eyes of the monkey. "Monkey get off dog at once, hurry-scurry, boola-boola, chop-chop!''

He didn't seem to understand. Instead of following my order, he flicked the end of my nose with his finger. And grinned down at me. That flicking business hurt.

I tried another tack. "Monkey not understand. Monkey get off and. . . .'' He flicked my nose again. "Monkey BAD monkey to flick master's nose with finger. Monkey be good monkey, get off and. . . ." He did it again.

"I don't think he speaks that language, Hank. He keeps flicking your nose."

"So it seems, Drover, and now I have no choice but to translate my message into the universal language—brute force."

"Oh gosh, don't hurt him."

"I'll try to be gentle, but I can't make any promises."

I took a deep breath and concentrated all the muscles in my highly conditioned body into an upward surge. Within a period of only a few seconds, I struck him in the chest with my front paws, kicked him in the back with my hind paws, and arched my back like a bucking horse.

G.L. Holmes

Pretty impressive, huh? But you know, these monkeys are used to living in trees and it's a little hard to shake one loose. I struggled and thrashed until I could struggle and thrash no more. The fool monkey was still sitting on my chest.

And you might say that he had, well, pinned my front legs to the ground, so to speak.

"Oops," said Drover. "That didn't work too well."

"It's just a simple language problem, Drover, nothing to be alarmed about. The little brute thinks I want to play with him. I'll have to use a sterner tone of voice, that's all." I narrowed my eyes and made teeth at him and snarled. "Monkey unpin legs right now, chop-chop, or face disastrous consequence!"

He unpinned my legs. I winked at Drover and gave him a smile. "There, you see? You can't monkey around with a monkey. You've got to be firm." I turned back to the monkey. "Now, monkey get off and wugg lum wum lum. . . ."

The little snot had reached into my mouth, taken hold of my tongue, pulled it out a full six inches, and was. . . .

Did I mention that one of the dangers of revealing Top Secret . . . yes, I did, and just as I had feared. . . .

"Oh, my gosh, Hank, he's got your tongue!"

"Wugg lumwum lum wugg!"

"I can't understand what you're saying."

"Wugg lum wugg wum lum wugg!"

"Do you want the monkey to turn loose of your tongue?"

"Uhhh!"

At that moment, the monkey spoke for the first time. "My name is not Minkey. I am Pasha of Shizzam, Lord Temporal and Spiritual, and heir to the throne of Raj Kumari."

Drover's eyes widened and he took two steps backward. "Oh my gosh, he's talking, Hank! And did you hear what he said?"

"Uhhh lum wugg wum."

The monkey looked at Drover. "Tell your friend that he weel not geet his tongue back until he recognizes that he ees a lowly subject of the Pasha of Shizzam. You weel tell him that."

"I will?"

"Indeed, you weel."

"What if I go hide in the machine shed?"

"If you go hide in thees machine shed place, I weel follow you and pool **your** tongue."

"Just thought I'd ask." He came creeping over and whispered in my ear. "Hank, did you hear?"

"Uhhh."

"I guess we'd better do what he says."

"Uhhh."

Just then, the monkey released my tongue and said, "Are you ready now to be a loyal subject of the Pasha?"

"Funny that you should ask," I said in bold tone of voice. "Number One, you're not a Pasha; you're a monkey. Number Two, I'm in charge of the ranch and wugg lum wugg wum lum wugg. . . ."

He sat there on my chest, grinning down at me and holding on to my tongue. "Perhaps you would like to try eet again?"

"Uhhh." He gave my tongue back. I rolled it around in my mouth and licked my chops. "As I was saying, we could probably work out some kind of compromise."

The monkey—eh, the Pasha—wagged one hairy little finger in front of my nose. "No compromise. I am Pasha, you are lowly, stinking, unwashed subjects."

"Yes, well . . . that sounds like the kind of compromise we could go for, so to speak. Now, if you'll get off my. . . ."

"You must obey Pasha or bad things weel come."

"Yes, of course."

"You promise obey Pasha? Or shall Pasha

seize tongue again?"

"Well, no, let's not get . . . I think we could probably. . . ."

"Promise or not promise!"

"Oh. I, uh, guess that we could take that under . . . all right, you win. We promise."

And with that, he crawled off my chest and let me up. That was his first mistake, letting me up, because I had already devised a clever plan for tabing the turnals on this upstart monkey. Turning the tables, I should say. For you see, I had begun drawing on my reserves of Ancient Cowdog Wisdom:

If at first you don't succeed, bark.

If at second you don't succeed, run for the house.

And that's just what we did, fellers, ran for the house. My monkey had gotten out of control and had decided that he was hot stuff. But he had never gone up against my favorite ranch wife, Sally May.

And I had a feeling that when Sally May got through with him, he'd have enough broom tracks on him that he'd forget about being the Pasha of Shizzam.

9

ATTACKED BY A NAKED WOMAN

Before the monkey could take defensive measures, we went streaking towards the house. When we came to the yard fence, I sprouted wings, fellers, jumped that fence like a deer, landed safely on the other side, and didn't slow down until I was standing on the porch, pressing against the screen door.

Drover was just a few steps behind. "We made it, Hank, we pulled it off!"

"Yes, we did, and nice work. I think Sally May will be proud of us for this one, Drover. Now we sound the alarm and alert the house. Bark, Drover, as you've never barked before!"

Boy, did we bark! We bristled the hair on our backs and lifted our heads and leaned into our barking. Loper had already gone for the day, but I knew Sally May was there.

The door opened and Little Alfred, age four, came toodling out into the utility room. He was wearing red and white polka-dot pajamas. His eyes were still puffy with sleep and he had an easy grin on his face.

"Drover," I said, "if we can coax him to open the screen door, we'll take refuge in the house."

"But what if Sally May. . . ."

"As long as we stay in the utility room and remain quiet, she'll never know we're there."

"I'm scared of Sally May."

"All right, I'll go into the house and you stay out here and entertain the Pasha of Shizzam."

"I think I'll go inside."

"I thought maybe you would."

Little Alfred came to the screen door and grinned down at us. "Hi, doggies, what ya doing?"

In the security business, there are certain techniques we use for begging our way into areas that are off limits. We whine, wag our tails, whimper, quiver, hop up on our back legs, and scratch on the screen with our paws.

If you've never seen a highly trained, well-conditioned cowdog going through the Heavy Beg maneuver, you'll just have to take my word for it. It's very impressive.

Little Alfred's mother, had she come to the door, would have provided a stern test of our ability. She was a hard sell. Her heart must have been whittled out of petrified wood. But Little Alfred was younger, kinder, and more pliable, and he also happened to be a special pal of mine.

When he came to the screen door, I called in all the old IOU's. I mean, this was an emergency situation and I put our friendship on the line. I put enough heavy begs on him to break his heart four times, and you know what? He opened the screen door and let us into the utility room.

Under ordinary conditions, I would have been satisfied to remain out in the utility room, along with the muddy boots, overshoes, old smelly gloves, chaps, spurs, and so forth. But this was a serious deal, and while the utility room was probably safer than the outside, it wasn't quite as safe as the house itself, with its thick walls and lockable doors.

Hence, when I saw that Little Alfred had left the door into the house ajar . . . well, it occurred to me that he probably **wanted** us to take refuge inside the house. That made perfectly good sense. I mean, here was a kid who realized the value of his dogs and wasn't about to take any chances with them.

These kids will surprise you, how sharp they are.

So I scrambled through the door and entered the house. Right away, I faced a decision: Which way to go? I was standing in the hall, don't you see, with the kitchen to my right and the bathroom to my left.

It was common knowledge that at this hour of the day, Sally May would have finished cleaning up the breakfast dishes and moved into the living room, where no doubt she would be playing with Baby Molly on the floor or reading a magazine.

Now that we were safe inside the house, warning Sally May about the monkey seemed less important in the overall scheme of things than hiding from her. After all, she had been known to throw dogs out of her house for no apparent reason.

A turn to the right would lead to a confrontation with her in the living room. A turn to the left would lead us into the bathroom where no one would think of looking for us.

So, naturally, I chose to go left instead of right. "Come on, Drover, into the bathroom!"

Only later did I discover that Drover didn't

86

follow me into the bathroom. Only later did I realize why.

The bathroom door was open a crack and I went plunging inside, throwing the door back against the bathtub with such force that it made a loud WHACK. This was followed by a woman's scream. "AAAAAAAAAAAAAAAH !" Huh?

By George, there she was in the bathtub, taking a bath. With Baby Molly. Instead of playing with her on the living room floor. Where she should have been. At that hour of the. . . .

Her scream tipped me off that I had invaded a lady's privacy and given her a scare in the midst of her bath, and that perhaps I wasn't welcome in there. By the time I realized the error of my ways, I had motored out into the middle of the tile floor. Hard tile, very slick, made changing directions something of a problem.

It was at that point that Sally May nailed me on the nose with a wet washcloth and exclaimed, "GET OUT OF MY BATHROOM, YOU FILTHY DOG!"

Let me pause here to point out that, while I **was** in her bathroom and I **was** a dog, as she had noted, I was NOT filthy. That very morning, only hours before, I had cleansed myself in the overflow of the septic tank, and we're talking about a complete emersion up to the tips of my ears.

I might have carried a few random particles of dust on my body, but we must remember that dust comes from God's good earth. If dust comes from dirt and dirt comes from the ground, then it follows that her charge was groundless.

Well, Sally May was a strong-armed ranch woman with a history of throwing rocks with deadly accuracy, and even sitting down in the bathtub, clutching a towel to her chin, and holding a baby in her lap, she could deliver a stinging blow with a wet washcloth. That thing hurt, and it also blinded me, since it draped across my nose and covered up my eyes.

I hit right full-rudder, reversed all engines, spun around in a circle, fell down three times on the tile, and got the old bod lined up with the door.

I throttled down hard and took aim at the open door, with every intention of getting the heck out of there.

I'll never understand why Little Alfred **closed the door on me.** Surely the kid . . . I mean we were friends, right? Good pals, tight

SPLAT

G.L. Holmes

buddies. We'd played together and hiked together and laughed together, and I can't believe that he would have locked me in there with his mother, knowing full well that. . . .

On the other hand, the boy did have his ornery side. I noticed that a certain sparkle came to his eyes, like a match lit in total darkness, and that a nasty little smile leaped across his mouth. Hmmm, yes.

But the long and short of it was that I, blinded by a wet washcloth, went scrambling for what I supposed was an open door, only to find it closed. Did it hurt when I rammed the door? Yes, it did, but not nearly as badly as the bar of soap that Sally May sent whistling across the room. Like most of her shots, this one went straight home, got me right in the ribs.

Clutching the towel to her chin, her hair in disarray and her eyes revealing destructive thoughts, she rose from the water like a sea monster.

"GET OUT OF MY BATHROOM! HIKE! GIT! SHOO! SCAT!"

Hey, she wanted me out of her bathroom? Not nearly as badly as I wanted to get out, but it just so happened that she had raised a hoodlum child who got his laughs by locking innocent dogs up in bathrooms with insane naked women.

Sally May threw on her housecoat and began flogging me with the towel. Near panic, I went sliding around the bathroom, looking for an exit or a hole to climb into. Somehow the trash can got knocked over and the toilet seat fell down with a crash and towels and washcloths fell from their proper places.

Suddenly the door opened and Little Alfred's face appeared. "Hi, Mom, what ya doing?" The grin on his face told it all—the little skunk had engineered this disaster and had been watching the entire show through the keyhole.

But the weed of crime bears bitter fruit. The boy had not only pranked me, but he had pranked one of the toughest, smartest, and meanest ranch wives in Ochiltree County.

"Did you let that dog in the house? And then lock him in my bathroom?"

She didn't wait for an answer but snatched him up, turned him over her knee, and frailed his little bottom. I paused for a moment to enjoy the first squalls from the little hoodlum, then I seized this opportunity to run for my life.

10

DEMOCRACY IN ACTION ON THE RANCH

Within seconds, I had made a pass through the house and taken cover in the darkness beneath Sally May's bed. It was a tight squeeze, but I managed it.

In the darkness, I listened to the rumble of battle. Sally May had wrung a full confession out of Little Alfred and he had been thrashed for it. Justice had been served.

"Now get your clothes on, Alfred. I have a dental appointment in forty minutes. And find that dog and throw him out!"

Throw ME out of the house? I had news for Little Alfred. There was no way he was going to haul me out from under the bed and throw me outside with that monkey. I had made a new discovery about monkeys, don't you see.

I didn't like 'em at all.

I had these thoughts on my mind when I heard a voice: "Hi, Hank. Did you get in trouble with Sally May?"

It was Drover's voice, and it was very near. My eyes probed the darkness and saw only darkness

"Are you under this bed?"

"Yeah. Are you?"

"Of course I am, and for very good reason. I was being flogged by a naked woman with a wet towel. What's your excuse?"

"Well, it sounded like things were getting hot in the bathroom and I thought. . . ."

"You thought you'd take the chicken's way out and hide under the bed, right?"

"Well . . ."

"And so you left one of your former friends to be mauled in a locked bathroom. I don't suppose it ever occurred to you to stick around and help, did it?"

"Well, yeah, it did occur to me, but I thought it was a pretty bad idea."

"This will go on your record, Drover, and believe me, it will not go unpunished."

"Oh drat. But anyway, we're safe from that crazy monkey. I knew he'd end up causing trouble."

"Yes, and so did I, Drover. I hope you've learned a lesson from all of this."

"I guess I have. Never trust a monkey in a red hat?"

"Exactly. And furthermore . . ."

Suddenly I heard footsteps on the floor. Small feet wearing shoes. Little Alfred was looking for us. We froze, hardly daring to breathe or move a muscle. The footsteps came into the bedroom and moved about. They stopped beside the bed. I held my breath and waited.

The boy's eyes appeared beneath the dust ruffle. They seemed to be upside-down. Yes, of course they were, since he had tilted. . . . I thought we were goners because he looked straight at me, but apparently it was too dark under there for him to see us.

The eyes disappeared, the footsteps moved into the living room, and Little Alfred said, "Mom, I can't find the doggies."

Sally May was crashing around in the other end of the house. "Well, we don't have time to look. We've got to leave right this minute. If those dogs make a mess, I'll. . . ."

She didn't finish her sentence, but she didn't need to. I had already made a mental note that, while in her house, we would make no messes.

When she came home, we would be lying on the rug beside the back door, minding our own business and guarding her house against robbers and fiends. No messes, not even one. She would be SO proud of us!

I heard the back door slam. The car started and went roaring up the hill in front of the house. And then . . . silence. I inched my way out from under the bed.

"All right, Drover, you can come out now. The coast is clear."

"How can you have a coast without an ocean?"

"What?"

He sneezed. "I said, it sure is dusty under there. Tears up by siduses."

"Are you saying that Sally May doesn't clean under her beds? Are you suggesting that she isn't a good housekeeper? Get to the point, Drover."

He sneezed again. "I dodt doe the poid, but by dose is all stobbed up."

"Well, let me remind you that a stopped-up nose is a small price to pay for being safe inside the house, away from the monkey."

"I thought you two were frids."

"Me? Friends with a monkey? Drover, I never trusted the little whelp, not for a minute."

He sniffed his nose. "Thid what was all thad stuff aboud you being the Grade Gred Podendade?"

I glared at the runt. "Great Grand Potentate? I don't know what you're talking about. You must have been dreaming."

"Doe, I wasn't dreebig. You said you were the Grade Gred Podendade, and the bucky was your Captain of the Guards."

"Rubbish. Come on, let's make a pass through the house and check things out. We're in charge now."

I crept out of the bedroom, peeked out the door, looked around in all directions, and started into the living room to give it a security sweep.

Drover was behind me, walking on tip-toes and checking things out with big moon eyes. "Hake, can buckys oben doors and cub into houses?"

I stopped. "What?" He repeated the question. Translated into common, non-sinus language, it meant, "Hank, can monkeys open doors and come into houses?" It was your typical dumb Drover-type question.

"Don't be ridiculous. We're safe inside the house, and I wish you'd stop asking silly questions."

"Whad's the edser?"

"The answer, which is obvious to everyone but you, is no, monkeys cannot now and never have been able to open doors and come into houses."

"How do you doe?"

"I know because . . . because it's the law, Drover. Or if it's not, it should be and will be. We live under a system of laws, not monkeys. No monkey is above the law and no law is below a monkey."

He ran his eyes around the room. "Baby so, but Hake, I'm feelig a little scared byself. I don't ever wad to see that bucky again."

"Nor do I, but that's my whole point, Drover. The law is here to protect us, to give us feelings of security, right? And laws are made by mature, responsible individuals, right? Hencely, we will put the democratic system to work and pass a law against monkeys."

"Well I'll be derd. I devver would have thought of that."

I gave him a fatherly smile. "Which is only one of many reasons why you're not Head of Ranch Security. Come on, let's get this thing signed into law and then we can relax. I'll give you a little lesson in government."

We went into the living room and I hopped up in that big rocking chair over by the east window, just below the hanging plant. I told Drover to sit on the floor in front of me.

I cleared my throat and struck a dignified pose. "The chair will now entertain a motion from the floor."

Drover gave me a blank stare. "You mean, that chair's going to dance on the floor?"

"No, that's NOT what I mean."

"Well, you said 'entertain,' and I just thought. . . ."

"Are you trying to make a mockery of our system of government? To hold a proper election, we must have a chair that recognizes a motion from the floor."

"I never heard of a chair that could recognize anything."

"Forget about the chair, Drover. It's just legal terminology. Now, you make a motion from the floor."

After giving me another blank stare, he stood up and walked around in a circle. "How's that?"

"What are you doing?"

"Making a motion. I guess. I don't know what I'm doing."

"No, incorrect, absolutely wrong. A motion from the floor, Drover, is whatever it is that we're fixing to vote on."

"Oh. Well, I'll vote for that."

"Not yet! We still don't have a motion, you brick."

"Well, how much emotion do you want?"

Sometimes . . . oh well. I managed to hold my temper. "Drover, listen to me. Don't think. Just say your part."

"I don't know my part."

"Hush and listen. When the chair calls for a motion, you will say, 'The floor moves that

100

monkeys cannot possibly open doors or enter houses.' That's all there is to it. Are you ready?"

"I guess."

"All right. The floor is open to motions." I waited and got nothing from Drover. "Well?"

"Is that chair really going to talk to me?"

"NO! I am the chair and you are the floor."

"This is crazy."

"Just say your lines, Drover."

"Okay. Let's see: 'The floor is moving around and monkeys can't come into this house.' "

"That's close enough. The floor has made the motion and the chair will second it. All in favor say 'aye.' " We both said "aye." "Motion has carried by unanimous vote of all present. Congratulations, Drover, we have taken self government to the dogs."

"Sure looks that way to me."

"And as a result of this solemn action. . . ." All at once my right ear shot up and I cut my eyes to the side. "Did you hear something?"

"Yes."

"Describe the sound."

"Door opening and door closing."

Suddenly I noticed a certain dryness of mouth. "It must be the wind, Drover. Of course it was the wind. What else could it be?"

It appeared that Drover's eyes had begun to cross. "The monkey?"

"Impossible. There are laws against. . . ."

And then we heard the voice. "Duggies? Where are you, duggies? Pasha comes for you."

HUH?

11

PASHA BREAKS THE LAW AND OTHER THINGS

"**D**rover, it occurs to me that . . ." The dunce had fainted, I mean, flat out on the floor. ". . . that I am dreaming." I squeezed my eyes shut. "This is only a dream. I don't believe in monkeys and what's happening here is against the law and therefore impossible. I repeat, this is only a dream."

With that out of the way, I opened my . . . AND THERE HE STOOD!

Red hat, red jacket, big grin on his face, evil wickedness in his eyes, crooking his finger at me, telling me to . . . no way I was gonna . . . holy smokes, I was trapped!

I tried to dive under the couch. Nope. I ran around in a circle but found that I was just going in circles. I barked—squeaked, actually.

Sometimes dreams can be more real than . . . moisture on my leg? Not just moisture. Wetness. Water. I knocked over, or shall we say, the antique lamp on the end table fell over and crashed to the floor.

I took dead aim for the underside of Sally May's bed but didn't quite make it.

He grabbed me by the ears and shook my head so hard, it turned my eyeballs around backwards. Then he said, "I am Pasha of Shizzam, and you are my slave."

"You're a monkey's uncle and lum wum lum lum!"

He'd got me by the tongue, see. "Do not call me a minkey. I am not a minkey. I am Pasha!"

"Lum wum lum."

"You have taught Pasha good treek, sizz tongue of dug and pool hard. Good treek, yes? Pasha like treek!"

"Wum."

Drover let out a groan. "Oh my gosh, I just had a terrible dream! I was locked in a house with a monkey!"

Pasha released my tongue, swaggered over to little Drover, and booted him in the tail section. "Do not say minkey! Geet up and be slave for Pasha."

"Oh my gosh, it's HIM! I thought it was a

. . . Hank, what are we gonna do?''

"Get up and be a slave for Pasha, what do you think?"

"You mean . . ."

"I mean we've been captured by a mon . . . by the Pasha of Shizzam."

"But I thought we voted. . . ."

"You'd better do what he says, Drover, before you get your tongue yanked out by the roots."

Pasha glanced at me and grinned. "Ver-ry good you understand Pasha!" The smile slipped into a snarl and he raised one hairy little finger in the air. "Now you leesen to Pasha. Pasha ees hungry, want food very much."

"Yeah, well, if you'll open up that back door, Pasha, we'll run up to the machine shed and get you some dog food. Great stuff. Co-op. You'll really . . ."

He shook his head. "Pasha not eat dog food, you fool. Pasha want Pasha food."

"Yes, I see, Pasha food. In that case, I suggest you open up the refrigerator and check it out."

"What meaning is refrigerator? Pasha not know refrigerator."

"Here, follow me." I headed for the kitchen. Passing by Drover, I whispered, "Play along with him. I've got a plan.''

"Oh good!"

"Shhhh!" I marched into the kitchen and stood in front of the refrigerator. "Here you are, Your Worthy Worship."

Pasha's eyes lit up. "I like that, 'Your Worthy Worsheep.' Ees ver-ry good, yes?"

"Nothing but the best for our Pasha of Shizzam. Now, with your hands, you can open that door. That's right, just grab the handle and pull."

He pulled and the door swung open. My eyes darted over the contents until I found what I had hoped would be there. I pointed towards two amber bottles near the bottom.

My plan was beginning to unfold. You see, whilst the monkey was holding my tongue, I had remembered a song I had learned as a pup:

The monkey he got drunk

And jumped on the elephant's trunk.

The elephant sneezed and fell on his
    knees

And what became of the monk, the
    monk, the monk?

You get the picture? Pretty clever, huh? Sometimes I even scare myself.

The monkey—Pasha, that is—reached a hairy little hand into the icebox and pulled out one of the bottles. He shook it, put it up to his ear, rolled it around in his hands, and tried to take a bite out of it.

"Not good! Pasha not like thees. Too hard to chew."

"Eh, no, Your Majesty. You don't eat it. You twist off the lid and drink it in one big gulp."

Pasha grumbled around for a minute, then twisted the lid. It fizzed and spewed in his face. He didn't like that. "What ees thees thing that speets in Pasha's face?"

I chuckled. "That's soda pop, Pasha. You'll love it. Just gulp it down and you'll be the happiest monkey . . . oops."

He came over to me, and he didn't look too happy. "You said minkey. Pasha is not minkey. Pasha is Pasha!"

"Yes, well, uh, hush my mouth, I never should have. . . ."

"Steek out your tongue!"

Well, old stupid me had said the wrong word and now I was going to get another tongue twisting, but that was okay because my plan was working to perfection. I opened my mouth, stuck out my tongue, and prepared myself. . . .

HUH?

I was definitely surprised when the monkey

stuck the bottle in my mouth and turned it up. I mean, I thought he was going to . . . sure was fizzy and foamy, and I can't say I liked the taste of it very much, but I either had to swaller it or drown.

I swallered and then did some serious burping.

The monkey pitched the empty bottle over his shoulder and gave me a smile. "Now! Eef thees ees poison, you weel die and Pasha weel watch."

For some reason, I started laughing. "No, it ain't pashion, Poisha, just a little old bottle of soda pop. You'll see, won't he, Djrover?"

"Hank, you're sure talking funny."

"Huh? Spick up, son, you're mumbering. Say, did anyone ever tell you that you have two heads and two faces? 'Cause you do."

"Hank, are you feeling okay?"

"Huh? Never fell better in my whole life, Djrover, just seeing double, izall." I turned my bleary eyes to Pasha. "You know what? You look juss slike a monkey to me."

His eyebrows shot up and a grin curled on one side of his mouth. "Eet ees not poison. Eet ees something else."

"You better believe it, Charlie, and I don't belief yer monkey enough to djrink one lum wum wugg lum."

He grabbed my tongue, pulled it out with one hand, and spanked it with the other. "I am not a minkey, you weel not call me a minkey, but I weel drink one nevertheless."

Whilst I was getting my tongue sorted out and stuffed back into my mouth, he reached in, got the second bottle, twisted off the cap, turned it up, and chugged it down.

He pitched the empty bottle over his shoulder and it crashed into a thousand pieces on the floor. He burped and shook his head.

"Eet does not work for me. I feel nothing. Now I weel find something else to itt."

He turned back to the refrigerator and fell into the second shelf, amongst the fresh spinach leaves and radishes from Sally May's garden.

I thought that was about the funniest thing I'd ever seen. I laughed like a fool, so hard I stumbled into the kitchen table and, well, sort of knocked the jelly jar and sugar bowl off on the floor.

Old Pasha climbed out of the spinach and came up wearing a big silly grin. "Eet ees very strange, thees soda pop stuff."

Oh, I howled at that! Laughed like crazy, right up to the moment when the first egg hit me between the eyes. "Hey, are you throwing eggs at me? Somebody around here's throwing . . ." SPLAT! ". . . eggs at me." SPLAT!

"I deed eet!" Pasha laughed. "'Twas I who threw theem."

"Why, you sorry outfit," I was laughing so hard I could barely talk, had egg dripping down into my eyes. "I'll fix yer wagon."

I swept my paw through the jelly that had spilled on the floor and rubbed it into Pasha's face and hair. Howling with laughter, we wrestled around, rolled into the refrigerator, and somehow managed to collapse a couple of shelves, which explains how a gallon of milk ended up spreading across the kitchen floor. . . .

Drover was about to have a seizure. "Oh my gosh, Hank, no, stop, the floor, Sally May's going to kill us all!"

"Oh dry up, you little squawk box, she'll never suspect a thing."

Pasha and I ended up on the bottom shelf, with our arms around each other's shoulders. We had become the best of friends, is what had happened, in spite of the differences between us.

He gave me a crooked smile. "I haff a confession to make. I am really a minkey, not a

Pasha. In circus, I do treeks and beg for money. I am only a beggar minkey."

"No kiddin'? Well, I have a confession to make too. I'm really a dog but I love this monkey business. I also love to sing, and I have an idea for a song about monkey business."

His eyes lit up. "You like to sing, yes? Maybe we sing together, yes?"

"You got a deal, pardner! Come on, Drover, let's tune up and knock the socks off of this song."

Drover had placed one paw over his eyes. "Hank, Sally May's going to kill us!"

CHAPTER

12

THE FIRING SQUAD

Monkey Business

Now, every creature on this earth
Needs a business to prove his worth,
Something to test his skills and express
   himself.
You've got plumbers and cowboys and
   carpenters,
Butchers, bakers, and saw sharpeners,
Guys who sack up groceries and stock
   the shelves.

Your business kind of sets the tone
Of who you are and how you're known.
And it's pretty important to pick one
   you understand.
So get yourself a business, son,

If you ain't there yet, I'll tell you one.
And you'd better buy stock in this one
    while you can.

Monkey business, monkey fun,
Monkey room for everyone.
Enroll yourself today in monkey school.
We've got a booming business here.
Depression-proof, owned free and clear.
And all you've got to do is act a fool.

Your local Better Business folks
Will probably tell you funny jokes
And call our line of work a big charade.
But the joke's on them, it seems to me,
When the truth's so very plain to see,
That monkey business is everybody's
    favorite trade.

So eat your heart out, Wall Street
    smarties,
Take GM, we'll take our parties,
And in ten years we'll just see what
    we've done.
We'll have show-and-tell, we'll have a
    quiz,
I'll put my dough on monkey biz

'Cause fools outnumber wise men ten to
   one.

   Monkey business, monkey fun,
   Monkey room for everyone.
   Enroll yourself today in monkey school.
   We've got a booming business here,
   Depression-proof, owned free and clear,
   And all you've got to do is act a fool,
      oh yeah.

   You've got to play this game by funky
      monkey rules, oh yeah.
   In monkey business, boys, just act a
      fool.

Well, me and my monkey pal sang the heck
out of that song, had us a big time. We not
only made a great contribution to music and
culture, but we also notched up a few points
for the Brotherhood of All Animals.

I mean, there I was, a very important dog,
socializing with a low-class monkey who went
around begging nickels in the circus. The fact
that I would stoop so low made my heart swell
with pride and almost brought tears to my
eyes.

One of the advantages of being wonderful is

that you can share it with others. Gives you a warm feeling inside.

Well, me and Monkey had a great time together, but old Sour Puss Drover sat through the whole thing and didn't sing a lick. When we finished, instead of cheering and shouting, as any intelligent dog would have done, he started whining and moaning.

"When Sally May comes home, your monkey business is going to get us killed!"

I glanced around the kitchen. It was a little messy, now that he mentioned it.

"Relax, Drover. We've got plenty of time. We'll get us a bite to eat and clean this mess up. Then our pal Monkey will open the back door for us, and we'll all vanish into the sunset, so to speak. Right, Monk?" He nodded. "See? Nothing to worry about."

"Hank, I want out now. I'm scared."

"Okay, fine, and who cares anyway? Monk, go open the back door and let the runt out so he can play chicken with the chickens."

Monk nodded, and they went to the back of the house. While they were gone, I turned to more important business. Among the items that had, uh, somehow spilled out of the open refrigerator was a package of, hmmm, hamburger.

I gave it a good sniffing. Sure smelled good. Fresh meat. Of course, I knew that Sally May had thawed it out for the supper meal and I wouldn't have dreamed of . . . but on the other hand, hamburger doesn't keep well at room temperature and. . . .

I found my nose nuzzling at the wrapping paper. You know, I was sniffing it out and, by George, would you believe that the wrapping paper just fell off, leaving two pounds of fresh, juicy hamburger exposed to germs and dangerous microbes and. . . .

Have you ever stopped to think how dangerous microbes are to little children? Very dangerous, and once germs have lit on a two-pound package of hamburger, it's next to impossible to get rid of 'em.

About the only precaution you can take is to eat the hamburger right away, and I mean all of it. Otherwise, you'll have plague and disease and sick kids laying around everywhere.

Well, you know where I stand on the issues of plague and disease. I'm 100% against 'em, and if I had my way, I'd abolish 'em completely. If a dog can't—this is for the record and you can quote me—if a dog can't protect the kids on his ranch from plague and disease, by George he ain't much of a dog.

117

So, in a selfless effort to save the ranch from an outbreak of deadly microbosis, I began disposing of the infected meat in large gulps.

I heard the door slam, then footsteps on the floor. "Hey, Monk, come here, son. I've got something. . . ."

Those were pretty heavy footsteps . . . for a monkey . . . I began to get this funny feeling . . . that I was being . . . stared at . . . you know how you get that feeling sometimes?

Very slowly, I turned my head away from the pool of hamburger blood on the floor and the wreckage of the refrigerator and the busted eggs and the jelly smears, and I'd sure expected her to stay longer at the dentist office.

That dentist sure hadn't done much . . . you'd think. . . .

I, uh, whapped my tail on the floor and tried to squeeze up a smile. She was probably about to jump to a hasty conclusion. That was my impression. I could heard the air rushing through her nostrils, and suddenly her eyes. . . .

Where were my friends when I really needed them?

I'd be the first to admit that Sally May and I had experienced our ups and downs. No relationship is easy. But never in my wildest dreams would I have thought that she would chase me around the house with hands that had become like claws.

Or drag me out from under her bed, or take a loaded shotgun from the bedroom closet. Or tie a blindfold around my eyes, carry both me and the gun down to the corrals. Or line me up against the fence and take up a position twenty paces away.

Never in my wildest dreams. . . .

The drums began to roll. "Ready!" I heard the hammers click on the shotgun. "Aim!"

"Wait, Sally May, I think I can explain everything. There was this monkey, see, who escaped from the circus and turned into a terrible despotic Pasha . . ."

"Lies, lies!"

"No, it's true, honest. And he forced strong drink upon me and made me do monkey business and terrible things, and never in my wildest dreams. . . ."

"Hank? You'd better wake up, I've got some bad news."

"Drover, when she pulls that trigger, all the bad news will be bad, because. . . ."

HUH?

Drover?

I pried my eyelids open and stared at the

runt. "Why, you traitor! You back-stabbing, two-faced snake in the grass! You left me in the kitchen to face the firing squad alone!"

"Firing squad in the kitchen? What are you talking about?"

I cut my eyes from side to side. It appeared that I was lying on my gunny sack bed, under the gas tanks. The sun was shining and, best of all, I saw no traces of Sally May or her shotgun.

With each new piece of evidence, it became clearer and clearer that I had just awakened from an incredible dream.

I pushed myself up on all-fours and staggered around, waiting for the fog to lift, so to speak, from the area between my eyes and whatever it is that resides behind the eyes.

Brain. Mind. Data Control Center. Whatever.

"Drover, let me ask you a question. To your knowledge has there ever been a monkey on this ranch?"

"Oh, yeah. He was in a box and the box fell off the back of a circus truck."

"Okay, that checks out. Question Two: Did this alleged monkey ever reach into your mouth and pull out your tongue?"

"He sure did, after you taught him to do it."

"Strike that from the record. I asked about

the monkey, not about me."

"Oh. Yeah, he pulled my tongue. He was a mean little cuss."

"That checks out too. Now, Question Three: Did this alleged monkey follow us into the house, present himself as an imposter called the Pasha of Shizzam, and force me to drink a bottle of beer?"

He stared at me and twisted his head. "That sounds crazy to me. I think you must have dreamed it."

"Yes, that checks out too. I remember saying over and over, 'Never in my wildest dreams.' But it WAS in my wildest dreams, Drover. Do you understand what this means?"

"It means you were dreaming, I guess."

"Exactly. And I won't be shot after all! Oh, happy day, Drover. The very best kind of day is one in which you know you won't be shot by a firing squad."

"Never thought about that, but Hank, I've got some bad news. While you were asleep, a man from the circus came by and got his monkey. He's gone."

I'm sure Drover didn't understand my spasm of insane laughter, since he hadn't participated in my dream. It took me several minutes to get control of myself.

Then Drover went on. "I thought you'd be sad, but I can already see that you're not."

I filled my lungs with fresh, clean air and gave myself a good stretch. "Well, Drover, as usual, there's a lesson to be learned from all of this."

"All of what?"

"And I'll expect you to make a note of it and refer to it in the future. Never open strange boxes, Drover, and leave monkey business to the monkeys."

And with that, we went streaking out into the home pasture to bark at starlings and black-birds, and to guide our ranch safely through another day.